The Secret of the Fourth Candle

Patricia St John

Revised by Mary Mills

Illustrated by Gary Rees

Scripture Union

©Patricia M. St. John 1977
First published by Scripture Union 1978
This revised edition first published 2001, reprinted 2002

Scripture Union, 207–209 Queensway, Bletchley, Milton
Keynes MK2 2EB
Email: info@scriptureunion.org.uk
Website: www.scriptureunion.org.uk

ISBN 1 85999 511 X

Printed and bound in Great Britain by
Creative Print and Design (Wales) Ebbw Vale.

Scripture Union is an international Christian charity
working with churches in more than 130 countries,
providing resources to bring the good news about
Jesus Christ to children, young people and families and
to encourage them to develop spiritually through the
bible and prayer.

As well as our network of volunteers, staff and associates
who run holidays, church-based events and school
Christian groups, we produce a wide range of
publications and support those who use our resources
through training programmes.

Contents

Titles by Patricia M. St John
THE TANGLEWOODS' SECRET
TREASURES OF THE SNOW
STAR OF LIGHT
RAINBOW GARDEN
THE SECRET OF THE FOURTH CANDLE
THE MYSTERY OF PHEASANT COTTAGE

For older readers:
NOTHING ELSE MATTERS
THE VICTOR
I NEEDED A NEIGHBOUR

For younger readers:
THE OTHER KITTEN
FRISKA, MY FRIEND

Revised edition

It is over twenty years since the first edition
of Patricia St John's The Secret Of The Fourth
Candle was published.
It has been reprinted many times and has become
a classic of its time.

In this new edition, Mary Mills has sensitively
adapted the language of the book for a new
generation of children, while preserving Patricia
St John's skill as a story teller

The Four Candles

The First Candle

It was still early morning and Aisha stood in the doorway of her home, watching the bright winter day break over the sea. The air was cold but very, very clear – so clear that she could even see the Rock of Gibraltar sitting in the sea like an old lion. The rising sun threw a silver path of light across the water, so that it looked to Aisha as though she could run across to it and spring on its back. Then her gaze wandered homewards, past the sparkling waters of the harbour, and came to rest on the house in the middle of the town where her mother went to work four days a week.

She had heard so much about that house that it was difficult to believe she had never been inside it, and still more difficult to believe that she had never met the fair-haired child with the strange foreign name who lived there. Aisha knew so much about her – what time she got up in the morning, what she had for breakfast and the colours of the many dresses she wore. She knew that this little girl went to school with her nurse every day, and played in a room full of books and toys. Her mother, who cleaned the nursery, told her about it nearly every day, and Aisha never, never got tired of hearing about it.

So when Aisha wasn't making bread, or

sweeping the house, or fetching water from the well, or chasing the goat or grinding the flour, or washing the clothes, or pulling the babies out of mischief, she liked to stand in the doorway and dream about the little girl in the big white house.

"Aisha," called her mother's voice quite calmly, "you had better come with me and help me today, and Safea must look after the little ones as best she can. It is Sunday, and on Sunday they have visitors and there is much cleaning and so many plates to wash up that I just can't manage alone. Why they can't all eat out of one dish like we do, instead of having three plates each and making all that work, I don't know!"

Aisha turned quickly, her cheeks bright pink, her eyes sparkling. For months she had begged her mother to let her go with her just once, and her mother had always said, "No, you must stay and look after the other children." Now her dream was coming true all by itself and she hadn't even asked! Too happy to speak, she ran to the bucket and scrubbed her face and hands till they shone, smoothed down her thick black hair and put a clean scarf over her head. She wished she had a clean cotton dress to match, but there wasn't one.

Now she was ready, dancing first on one foot and then on the other, whilst her mother gave final instructions to poor little Safea who was only seven years old and small for her age. "...and don't let the baby fall into the well," said her mother, "and don't let the goat get through the fence and don't let the cat drink the milk."

"Come on, mother, we shall be late," shouted Aisha, and danced off down the hill. She did not wish her baby to fall into the well, but the goat and cat could do what they liked. Nothing mattered today; she was going to fairyland. She skipped happily on, across the common where the donkeys grazed, on to the white road that wound between eucalyptus trees. Through a dip in the hills, the sea sparkled blue and silver, and the exciting noises of the town began to grow nearer.

They reached the broad Boulevard with its big shops all shut because it was Sunday. The white house where the little girl lived was at the far end of the Boulevard up a flight of marble steps. Aisha suddenly felt rather frightened and walked more slowly.

Her mother knocked at the front door, which was opened by another servant, and Aisha, with a beating heart, stepped over the threshold of her palace of dreams. It was a little bit disappointing; just a rather dark hall with a staircase leading upwards. She only had time to glance at it before she was bustled away into the kitchen and told to scrub the floor.

But she was not really disappointed, because, although the kitchen floor was very large to scrub, and Fatima the cook was very cross, she had seen the staircase, and at the top of the staircase lived the child with the golden hair. One day Aisha would tiptoe up very softly and see her, and they would smile shyly at each other, because, after all, they were both little girls.

The winter day sped by; Aisha wiped the dishes, scoured the pans, cleaned the dustbins and scrubbed the kitchen, and by that time dusk was falling. The street lamps burned on the Boulevards and the lights from the ships zigzagged in the purple waters of the harbour. Aisha, standing alone in the kitchen, her work finished, stretched her tired little body and stood listening. Her mother was cleaning some back yard and Fatima was comfortably asleep by the fire. She was quite alone. She tiptoed to the kitchen door, out into the passage, and stood, with her hands clasped and her face lifted, at the bottom of the staircase.

It was a long staircase, but at the top of it there was a door held open and a light shone out into the passage. It was a soft, friendly, welcoming light, and Aisha suddenly forgot to be afraid. She scuttled up the staircase toward it on silent bare feet, and peeped into the room.

A little golden-haired girl was standing by a table, and on the table was a wreath of evergreens with four white candles. Three of the candles had not been lit, but the fourth burned with a pure light, reflected in the starry eyes of the little girl.

It was the prettiest sight Aisha had ever seen in her life. For one moment she stood breathless, gazing, and then her mother's voice in the kitchen recalled her. She scuttled down the staircase as swiftly and noiselessly as she had scuttled up it and stood meekly waiting in the passage.

And her mother never knew that she had been to fairyland! She thought she had been standing in the passage all the time, and together they left the house and made their way up the lighted Boulevard, her mother grumbling at how late they were, but Aisha thinking only of that one pure white candle, and the starry eyes of the child reflecting its light.

The Second Candle

The week passed very quickly and Aisha worked as hard as usual, but somehow it was quite different from all the other weeks. She kept remembering that bright, flickering candle.

The question was, would she be allowed to go again? Things had not gone very smoothly while Safea had been left in charge. The goat had eaten the dinner and the cat had scratched the baby's nose. But on Sunday morning it was raining, and rain meant dirty floors and the passages to scrub several times a day. Aisha's mother had a headache and decided to risk leaving the baby again.

"Come along, Aisha," she said crossly as she draped herself in her big white cotton gown. "You'll have to help me again today whether you like it or not, and Safea, if you don't look after the baby properly I'll give you such a thrashing!"

Safea nodded calmly and went on munching her breakfast. The many thrashings her mother promised her children very seldom happened.

"Yes, mother, I'll come and help you," replied Aisha dutifully, and together they splashed their way down the slippery hillside and across the muddy common. Into the town, and up the marble steps and in at the front door they went, and once again Aisha scrubbed the great big kitchen and listened to Fatima's moaning and threats of what she would do to her if she broke anything. In fact the day passed exactly as the Sunday before, until just half an hour before it was time to go home. And then Aisha's adventures began.

The tea-tray with its pretty china cups had been carried downstairs; Fatima stood at the sink washing them and handing them to Aisha to dry. Her mother had disappeared into the back yard and it was getting dark. The child was very tired, and she kept thinking about the room upstairs with the lighted candle.

Crash! The china cup slipped from her hand and splintered into a hundred pieces on the stone floor.

Aisha jumped and then felt a hard blow on her

head. Furious Fatima was screaming with rage and her strong red hand was raised to strike the little girl again.

"You wicked little wretch!" she yelled, "and the mistress doesn't even know you are in the house. Your mother shall take the blame for this, not me."

Her hand came down hard, but Aisha dodged it and fled from the kitchen as swiftly as a little bird. She was almost blind with panic and fear and there was only one place in this great, cold, unfriendly house where she could be safe. She would run to where that little white flame burned comfortingly in the darkness. She disappeared into the passage, and Fatima, hitting her hand on the table instead of on Aisha, was too hurt to run after her for a moment or two. The door was open, and she supposed the child had escaped into the street, and went back to the kitchen snarling with rage.

Aisha ran straight to the staircase. She glanced up just once and saw the light of the open door, blurred through her tears, welcoming her. She sprang up the stairs like a frightened rabbit to its burrow, rushed into the nursery, slammed the door behind her and flung herself, sobbing and trembling, on to the floor at the feet of the little girl.

Petra stared at her in astonishment. She was a kind little girl and it troubled her to see a child no older than herself in such a sorry state. She longed to ask her what was the matter but unfortunately they couldn't speak the same language.

She thought it might, however, comfort her to see the lovely thing she had just been doing, so she poked the sobbing little girl on the shoulder until she looked up. Aisha stopped in the middle of a loud wail, took a deep breath, and stared and stared at the scene in front of her.

There was the table and the wreath of evergreens with four white candles. Two had not been lit but two burned with a clear white light, reflected in the happy eyes of Petra and in the tears of Aisha.

Two candles this week – and last week there had only been one! And Petra was smiling and pointing to them as though they had some happy secret to tell – some secret of peace and gentleness and stillness. She forgot the cold, unfriendly kitchen and cross Fatima, and her heart felt all warm and unafraid and she smiled back and drew closer to the little girl. Her dirty ragged skirt brushed against the beautiful white folds of Petra's dress, but neither of them noticed.

Suddenly lots and lots of questions rose up in Aisha's mind and she longed so much to be able to ask them, but she couldn't, so the tears welled up in her eyes again. Why did they light one the week before and two this week, and when would they light the third and the fourth, and what would happen when they were all alight? She pointed to the candles not yet lit and tried to get

Petra to light them.

But Petra shook her head very strongly. She looked quite shocked at such an idea.

But as they stood quietly by the table, the little princess of plenty and the ragged servant child, happy together, a step was heard coming down the passage, a horrid outside sound, spoiling the peace and safety that the candle-light seemed to bring. Aisha suddenly remembered with a start that she was not safe at all; she was a little trespasser who had pushed her way into a place where she had no right to be. Her eyes grew wide with terror and she bolted for the door and began to run down the dark staircase as quietly as she had come up it.

But Petra was as quick as she was. She was a very lonely little girl shut away in her grand nursery with no brothers or sisters, and the sudden appearance of a bright-eyed, tousle-haired stranger who crept into the magic circle of her candle-light was as good as an adventure in a story book. She must not let her disappear for ever like that. There was one language that they both probably understood a little, and that was Spanish. Petra darted to the top of the staircase and called softly after the flying figure:

"Venga – Domingo otro."
(Come again – next Sunday.)

Then she darted back just in time, and was

standing quietly by the table when Zohra, the nursery maid, a kindly woman who spoke some English, came in with the bucket of coals to make up the fire.

Zohra had not noticed Aisha's flying shadow on the staircase, nor did she guess Petra's secret. And Aisha's mother, worrying about the broken cup as they trudged homewards, knew nothing about the secret either. It was locked up tight in the hearts of the two little girls.

Aisha knew quite a lot of Spanish, and she had heard Petra's message and understood it perfectly.

And that week those words came into her mind over and over again –

"Come again – next Sunday."

The Third Candle

There was only one more Sunday before Christmas and the great shop windows on the Boulevard were wonderfully bright and cheerful. At sunset that evening Petra and her mother had lit the third Advent candle.

"And," said Petra, "when I light the fourth it will be time to hang up my stocking!"

Her mother laughed and kissed her and told her to run along because on Sunday night Petra's mother usually went to a party and she was in a hurry to be off. Petra clung to her for a moment. She loved the cool feel of her mother's dress and the sweet smell of her cheeks. If only her mother was not quite so pretty and popular she would not have to go to quite so many parties! Then she would have time to come up to the nursery and stand in the beautiful white circle of the three candles and talk about Christmas secrets. Now the car was at the door and her mother was off and away down the passage. Petra gave a little sigh and climbed the staircase alone, her evergreen wreath in her hand.

But she did not really mind about her mother tonight, because she was sure the funny little girl would come, and Zohra would talk to her in her own language and tell her all about the candles, and she would show her the Christmas presents all wrapped up in Christmas wrapping paper and put away in the drawer. She went in search of Zohra and the coal bucket.

"Zohra," said Petra in her most pleading voice, "I want you to stay with me tonight. I have a secret and you must help me."

Zohra was always ready to help her adored Petra, so she smiled, laid down her bucket of coals, and sat down by the fire to wait and see what would happen. She never knew with Petra. She sometimes had the strangest ideas.

"There is a little girl coming to see me," explained Petra importantly, "and she only speaks your language. I want you to tell her what

I tell you and I want to show her my Christmas presents."

This sounded innocent enough. Zohra smiled enthusiastically and nodded; probably, she thought, this was a little school friend, the daughter of some rich Moor, whose mother was bringing her to visit Petra.

But just at that moment there was a tiny rustle and movement, and the smile died on Zohra's face and she looked extremely angry. For round the door there appeared a tousled head wrapped up in an extremely dirty cloth, and a pair of bright anxious eyes set in a dirty little face. The bright eyes did not see Zohra at first. They gazed at the three candles burning on the table.

"There she is!" cried Petra joyfully, and she rushed to the door, dragged Aisha into the room, and slammed it behind her. "I *knew* you'd come," she said. "Look, I've lit the third candle!"

Aisha could not understand a word but she was delighted at the warmth of the child's welcome, and for a moment her face glowed with love and joy. Then it suddenly turned blank with fear for she had caught sight of Zohra in the shadows, and Zohra's face was certainly not welcoming. Aisha turned and made a dash for the door but Petra stood in the way and grabbed firm hold of her.

"You are not to run away!" she ordered her. "I am going to tell you all about my candles.

Zohra, you tell everything I say to this little girl, so she can understand it, in Arabic."

Zohra shook her head helplessly. She recognised Aisha – the dirty child who scrubbed the kitchen on Sundays. How the little creature had ever got into the nursery was more than she could understand, and she was quite sure Petra's mother would be very angry.

"Your mother wouldn't like it," she said in her broken speech. "You know she wouldn't."

"My mother's gone to a party," replied Petra impatiently. "Don't be silly, Zohra. Do what I tell you. This little girl is my friend. Tell her that I light one candle every week on Sunday night for the coming of the Baby Jesus. Tell her that next week is the feast of his coming. Tell her to be sure to come back next week and see, because on Sunday I shall light all four candles and hang up my stocking and then it will be Christmas."

Zohra sighed, but decided that the best way to get rid of this unwelcome little visitor was to do what Petra wanted. So she repeated the first two sentences in Arabic like a parrot, but she changed the last part of Petra's message.

"She says," explained Zohra, "that she lights one candle every week for the coming of the Baby Jesus and next week is the feast of his coming and she will light them all – but what you think you are doing here I don't know, you naughty little thing, and don't let me ever catch you in this nursery again or I'll hand you straight over to Fatima in the kitchen."

Aisha gazed at her sorrowfully and doubtfully. The three candles were burning just as she had known they would be burning, but somehow it was all spoiled. There was someone who didn't want her there, and she felt afraid and wanted to run away.

But perhaps it didn't matter, because the little girl certainly did want her and the little girl was, after all, queen of the nursery. Petra suddenly took Aisha's hand and led her to a corner of the nursery and opened a drawer now full of presents wrapped up in bright Christmas paper.

"Tell her they are my presents, Zohra," commanded Petra, "presents for everyone in the house and all my uncles and aunts. And tell her that if she'll come again next Sunday I will have a present for her."

"She says they are her presents," interpreted Zohra, "and now for goodness' sake do get back to the kitchen and don't come up here again!"

She did not speak unkindly, for Aisha was a child of her own race, and probably meant no harm, but she was frightened of being in trouble herself if such a very dirty, greasy little creature was found in her Petra's nursery. If only she could get rid of her now, she would speak to Fatima about it before next Sunday. Fatima would certainly never let such a thing ever happen again.

Aisha looked in amazement at the candles, and

then back at the presents, and almost forgot Zohra. She knew at last why the little girl lit one more candle every week. It was in honour of a baby called Jesus who was coming next week, and then all the candles would burn and the whole room would be white and bright and the baby would be there laughing. She had never heard of Jesus before, but she felt sure he must be a very important baby to have the candles lit specially for his coming. And all those presents, too! She supposed they were all for him and she wondered what was inside them. She wanted to see him more than she had ever wanted to see anything else in the world. If only that woman would stop looking at her so crossly and spoiling it all. She suddenly looked at Zohra again, and felt frightened and shy. She gave one quick grateful smile at the little girl, dashed to the door and ran off down the stairs as swiftly and silently as before. But before she reached the bottom again the clear, urgent voice of Petra called after her.

"Venga – Domingo otro."

Aisha's mother was in a hurry to get back home that night but she had hard work in getting her daughter up the Boulevard. Aisha seemed lost in a dream, dawdling, pressing her nose against every shop window until her mother slapped her.

She did not mind much. There were such lovely things in the shops and although she hadn't any money of her own she wanted them all for the Baby Jesus. One great idea had come to her and she could think of nothing else. She would give him a present, too. Next Sunday she would creep upstairs into the room where the four candles would be burning. She would not stay – just see him for a moment, kiss his chubby hand and lay her present at his feet, and then slip back into the dark, satisfied.

The question was, what present could she take him?

The Gift

She thought of little else all that week. It rained nearly every day, the cold, torrential winter rain of North Africa, and the children crouched round a clay pot of burning charcoal and tried to keep warm. The goats and hens came into the house for shelter and got in the way and underfoot. The roof leaked, the baby coughed and wailed and snuffled, and everybody got on everybody else's nerves. It was a difficult week for everyone – except for Aisha, who nearly drove her mother crazy by being so dreamy and sitting gazing into the charcoal not noticing anything or anyone around her.

She saw wonderful pictures in the charcoal – pictures of herself kneeling in the candle-light, her hands piled with glittering gifts to lay at the feet of a loving, joyful baby, who stretched out his arms towards her. Sometimes, when she was asleep at night cuddled under a sheepskin with Safea, the baby came right into her arms and she felt, in her dreams, the warmth of his sturdy little body and knew that if she could only hold on to him, she would never be lonely or afraid again. Then she would wake up to the coldness of the grey morning, with the drip of the rain through the thatch, and realise that he was only a dream and she had empty hands, for after all, what could she take him?

Nothing – she had nothing at all! She stood in the doorway, feeling depressed, gazing outside, when her mother seized her by the shoulder and gave her a good shake.

"You do nothing all day but stand and stare," she shouted. "You are no more use in the house than a cow – and the baby has spilled the grain under your very nose! Now go to the well and bring me two buckets of water quickly and don't stand all the afternoon staring into the water."

She gave her a final push through the doorway and out into the grey rain. Aisha sighed and picked up her bucket and set off shivering. It was horrible going to the well in this weather, but there was nothing else to be done. She ran as fast as she could, clatter, clatter down the hill, but she couldn't run back. The hill was very steep and the buckets very heavy, and the pouring rain half-blinded her. Worst of all, she had no present for the baby. She was so miserable!

Walking with her head well down she bumped into old Msouda who was going to the well, grumbling, mumbling, moaning and shivering. Msouda lived in the hut next to Aisha and it was very hard for her to draw water at her age, but the orphan grandson who lived with her had broken his arm and there was no one else to do it. She was very angry with Aisha for pushing into her and Aisha was just about to be rude back when she noticed that the old woman was crying. Hopeless little sobs of weariness and cold and weakness came from under the scarf that covered her bowed head.

Aisha suddenly felt terribly sorry for her. She set her buckets down in a safe place by the side of the path and took Msouda's buckets out of her hands.

"I'll fetch your water, Msouda," she said. "You go back home." She turned back down the path leaving the old woman gaping with astonishment. When she returned, Msouda had gone into her hut and was busy looking for something under the bed.

Aisha set down the buckets in the doorway with a clatter and turned to go, but Msouda suddenly came out from under the bed and ran after her and thrust something soft and sticky into her hand.

"You are a good girl," she said, "and I'll give you one of my newly baked khaif."

Aisha stood quite still in the rain, staring at her treasure, her heart suddenly full of joy, because there is nothing babies like better than khaif. It is a sort of flat, flaky cake, made from flour and water, sprinkled in oil and baked on a flat pan.

She was so excited that she ran home as far as the bamboo fence without her buckets, and then suddenly remembered and had to go back for them. Fortunately her mother had not seen her. She walked back into the house as though nothing had happened, and nobody knew about her wonderful secret.

She had no pretty paper like Petra, but she chose a couple of flat shiny leaves and hid her khaif between them and placed it in a safe corner under the sheepskin. At night she took it to bed with her. It does not matter if you lie on top of a khaif because it is already flat.

Carrying it to town next day without her mother seeing was difficult, as Aisha's clothes were very thin and ragged. She laid it on top of her head and put a scarf over it and walked upright, very carefully. By the time she reached the big house she had a stiff neck and was glad to wrap the khaif up in her scarf and lay it in the corner of the kitchen. Then somehow she must live through the long hours of the day until the lights began to twinkle in the streets and she could run up the magic staircase and see the four candles burning and lay her gift at the feet of the baby.

She kept wondering if the baby had arrived yet and once or twice she tiptoed to the passage and listened for the sound of happy cooing or contented chuckling. But all was quiet and the door where the little girl lived was tight shut, so she didn't worry about it very much. Perhaps the baby was coming by ship and they had all gone down to the port to meet him.

Aisha's mother was busy as usual in the yard and Fatima had disappeared. Aisha was all alone in the kitchen and the moment had arrived for her to go and look for the baby. They would probably be lighting the fourth candle right now. Hope, love, fear, courage, wonder and longing, all flooded her simple little heart and drove her breathlessly into the dark passage, clasping the precious khaif tightly against her chest.

She tiptoed to the bottom of the staircase and looked up. The door was once more open and the soft, welcoming light streamed towards her – a little stronger and clearer than before because tomorrow would be Christmas and Petra had lit all four Advent candles.

It was very quiet. Perhaps the baby was asleep. Aisha, rosy with joy, scuttled up the staircase towards her fairyland.

But as she reached the top of the stairs a rough hand shot out and seized her by the arm, and too bewildered to cry out she found she was being hustled downstairs. Slapped and shaken, stumbling and gasping, she was at the bottom before she realised what had happened, and then the light from the kitchen shone on Fatima's furious face so terrifyingly near her own.

"Yes, I know all about it," snarled Fatima, who dared not make too much noise in the passage. "Zohra told me – sneaking upstairs right into my lady's room. I thought I'd just catch you at it tonight – you try that again – this is the end of you – I'll tell your mother about you." Slap! Slap!

Aisha, coming to her senses, gave a loud scream. Fatima clapped her hand over her mouth, pushed her through the front door and slammed it behind her. She was alone on the steps, still clasping her khaif to her heart.

She had no idea where she was going, but she must get away somehow from the terrible Fatima, and she started running down the bright, crowded Boulevards, bumping into people, noticing nothing, sobbing bitterly. But it was not the slapping or the shaking that she really minded – in fact she hardly thought about them at all. What really mattered was that she had not seen the baby. She had crept within a few yards of him. Without a doubt he had been there, fast asleep in a soft cradle, in the light of four candles, but the khaif that was to have been laid gently on his bed was still in her hand.

Aisha was so upset that she never heard the people shout or the policeman blow his whistle or the scream of brakes as she dashed blindly across

the road. Nor could she ever remember after-
wards being knocked over by the big car. She lay
unconscious in the road and the crowds gathered
round her, all chattering in different languages,
until the ambulance arrived and drove her to the
English hospital on the cliff overlooking the
Straits of Gibraltar.

The Baby

She did not wake properly till twilight the next
day because she had hit her head on the kerb and
concussed herself slightly; also her leg had been
broken by the wheel of a car. She had woken
during the afternoon, and thought she heard the
sound of singing very far away, and thought she
saw candles burning; but it might all have been a
dream.

But when she woke at dusk she knew quite well
she was not dreaming. She was wide awake and
her leg hurt her and she felt giddy and wondered
where she was. After a while she stopped wondering and just lay quite still, looking and listening.

She was lying on a raised bed, which was
rather frightening because she had always slept
on the floor. However, there was a whole row of
other people on raised beds and they did not
seem to be falling out, so perhaps it was quite
safe after all. At the other end of the room there

were groups of people all looking at a tree, and among the evergreen branches burned many candles. Round the tree stood a group of children in long, bright dresses, singing in Arabic –

"Away in a manger, no crib for his bed,
The little Lord Jesus lay down his sweet head."

Aisha's heart gave a sudden leap. "The little Lord Jesus" – that was the name of the baby who was going to stay with Petra, but it seemed he was here instead, for they were singing about him and had lit at least fifty candles in honour of his coming.

She fell asleep again and when she woke it was night and there were no candles – only one tiny red lamp glowing above the door, casting a dim light over the room. Nor was there any more singing – only the snoring of sleeping patients. Aisha lifted her head cautiously from her pillow and looked round. The night nurse noticed her and came over to see how she was feeling.

Aisha liked nurses. Just a year ago her baby brother had sat down in the clay bowl of red-hot charcoal and Aisha had carried him to this same hospital every morning for his dressings. The nurse had always been kind and pleased to see her and once she had stopped Absalom's screaming by giving him a pink sweet. Nurses were definitely friendly and could be trusted. Aisha smiled and kissed this one's hand by way of greeting.

"I want to see the baby!" said Aisha. "Where is he? Has he gone to sleep yet?"

"Which baby?" asked the nurse gently. "Do you mean your baby brother?"

"No, I don't," answered Aisha, "I mean the baby called Jesus. He was going to Petra's house and then he came here instead. The children sang about him and all the candles were lit. Where is he? I had a present for him but I don't know where it is now."

The nurse was puzzled. How had this little local child with her big, anxious black eyes heard of Baby Jesus? And who was Petra? She sat down on Aisha's bed and tried to explain.

"Aisha," she said, "you cannot see the Baby Jesus because he was born many years ago and now he has gone back to God. But the children were keeping the feast of his birthday and singing how he came into the world to save us from our sin and sadness. I'll tell you about him, Aisha, and then you'll understand."

Aisha lay very still, her dark eyes fixed on the nurse's face. She wanted to understand about the baby more than anything else in the world.

"God loved us, Aisha," said the nurse, "so he sent his Son Jesus to show us the way to heaven. He became a little baby like us. His mother was very poor and laid him in a manger when he was born. He has gone back to God now, but he is still alive and he still loves us. He is with us all the time although we can't see him and he can still show us the way to heaven."

She shook up the child's pillow and moved quietly away, and Aisha lay staring at the red glow of the tiny lamp, thinking, thinking.

She had imagined herself running into the light of that candle glow for one moment, flinging her gift at the feet of the baby, and then running back into the cold dark for ever. Now it was all different. He was not coming after all, and she would never see him; yet she was not unhappy, for the nurse had told her something even better.

"He loves you. He is with you all the time although you can't see him ... he will show you the way to heaven." That was what the nurse had said, and dreamily she imagined a long bright road winding through the darkness. At the beginning of the road stood a beautiful, bright-eyed baby. In one hand he clasped a lighted candle and with the other he beckoned her to follow him, and the love of his happy heart drew her towards him just as the glow of light had drawn her up the dark stairway. In her dream she ran to him and put her hand into his and knew that she had found everything she had ever wanted in her life. She knew that nothing need ever frighten her or hurt her again, because no one could take the baby from her or her from the baby. He offered her safety and love, shelter and happiness.

When all the Candles were lit

Aisha's leg was broken quite badly and she stayed in hospital six weeks and enjoyed every moment of it. But the highlight of the day was at three o'clock in the afternoon when her mother came to visit her, with the baby tied on her back and all the little brothers and sisters trailing behind. Then at seven o'clock at night the English missionary came with a guitar and they all sang songs and heard wonderful stories about Jesus when he was a man.

She loved hearing how he laid hands on sick people and made them better without any medicine at all, and on little children and sent them away happy and good and blessed. But one night the missionary told a very sad story of how those kind hands had been nailed to a cross of wood, and the Lord Jesus had been put to death. He had died willingly and lovingly to pay for all the wrong things that Aisha and everyone else in the world had done. This made Aisha very sorry, for she knew that she had often told lies and lost her temper and been rude to her mother and slapped the babies. She lay thinking about it for a long time, and once again she half dreamed, half imagined that Jesus came and held out his hands to her. This time she could see that they had been wounded and she knew that all the wrong things she had done could be forgiven and she could start all over again.

"All my life I'm going to follow Jesus on the path that leads to God," she whispered, clasping her small brown hands together. She loved him with all her heart and longed to give him a gift. She thought of beautiful little Petra lighting candles for his coming and wrapping up presents. She wished she too could light candles – but she couldn't. She was just a poor, ordinary child with nothing to give.

After a time she was given some crutches and allowed to leap around the garden, then she was allowed to walk alone with a stick – and one beautiful spring day the doctor told Aisha he was going to take her home that afternoon in his car.

She lay quietly thinking about it after he had gone. She couldn't be quite sure if she was pleased or not. It was not that she was going to say goodbye for good, because she was going to come back for Sunday school every week and bring Safea to visit all the nurses; but six weeks is a long time in the life of a little girl, and she had become used to the cleanliness and space of the hospital, and its ordered way of life. She had none of these in her family's cottage up the mountain. She thought of the goat, the babies, the cats, the overturned buckets of water, the charcoal smoke, the leaking roof on wet days and the washing that wouldn't dry, and she sighed a little. When the nurse asked her if she was excited about going home, she didn't answer.

The doctor arrived straight after dinner and hustled her off with the voices of the patients calling after her. "Visit us again, Aisha – go in peace and may God bring you happiness!"

She didn't have any luggage to carry, and waved to them with both hands as the car sped out of the gate. Then they were roaring up the mountain road, with the sea through the dip in the hills far below and the town far behind them.

The doctor, who had visits further up the mountain, set her down on the slope below her home and said goodbye, and for a few moments she stood there alone looking about her. Flowers were out along the stream bed and baby lambs skipped amongst them. The children suddenly saw her and came tumbling out of the cottage to meet her.

The next few minutes were just a bewildering jumble of shouts and laughter and hugs and kisses. Somehow she found herself sitting on the steps of her home with the baby on her lap, Absalom behind her with his hands clasped round her neck, Mustapha and Sodea, one under each arm beaming up at her and the goat butting her rather painfully in the back. Her mother made mint tea in honour of her home-coming, and Safea swayed about joyfully on one leg in front of her.

And Aisha, flushed and very, very happy, suddenly laughed out loud as she remembered the quiet, clean hospital ward and her lovely white bed. She wondered how she had managed to live for six weeks away from these hot, grubby, sticky hands of her little brothers and sisters. She looked down at the thin baby with its spotty head and runny nose and decided there had never been another baby quite so dear or beautiful. Her heart was almost bursting with love for them all, and she suddenly remembered and understood why.

She had come to know the other baby – Jesus. He was now living in her heart. She now saw everything around her in a clearer, happier light, and deep inside she felt at peace, and was glad to be home.

Like the light from the four Christmas candles, love, goodness, peace and joy shone out from Jesus, covering Aisha, the cottage, her mother and the grimy, happy faces of the children. They would all be safe in the glow of his love.

The Cloak

Morning

The grey light was creeping into the city streets when Mustapha woke up, shivered and pulled his ragged old cloak tightly round him. His face was covered by the hood, but he pushed it back just a little and peered round. He wanted to see what was happening but he didn't want to let in the draughts.

The other boys lay around, sleeping uneasily in the miserable café, where the air was still thick with last night's stale tobacco smoke. Dirty glasses stood on the tables and the boys were unwashed and homeless. Most of them lay huddled up, muttering about being cold.

Mustapha stared at them gloomily from under his hood. He had not been in the city long, and he hated the daily chilly wakening in this wretched place. It was not comfortable sleeping on the floor, but he was used to that, and at least while you were asleep you could forget about being hungry, dirty and homeless. Sometimes in his dreams he drifted back to the time, not so long ago, when he had lain down at night near his mother in their mountain home. He must have been dreaming about her that morning, for while he was still only half-awake he found himself thinking about her. She was a simple country-woman, but her love for him had been very strong. How often she had given him bread and gone hungry herself; perhaps that was partly why she had died so young. It was three years since he had seen the mountains near his home and he wondered what they looked like now – probably all under snow, with the strong winds sweeping down the ravines.

It was warmer in the city, but the mountain air had been clean and pure. He suddenly wrinkled his nose, got up with an expression of disgust, and made his way stiffly to the door.

The cold air of the street seemed to hit him and he trotted along fast, his teeth chattering. It was only 6am, but oh, how he wanted some breakfast! From the mosque nearby came the dawn prayer call, but Mustapha had never learned to pray. He had nowhere to go and nothing to do, and with his dream of the mountains fresh in his mind the streets seemed unbearable.

He would go down to the beach; there at least he would find clean breezes and wide spaces, and there he could run and get warm. He trotted down a broader alley with shuttered shops on each side. At the bottom was a stone jetty running out to a port where big ships lay anchored, and to the right stretched the long, curved sands of the bay. Sunrise flamed over the water and even Mustapha was struck by its beauty and stood wondering for a moment. It was so lonely – just himself, the seagulls and the little waves tinted with gold.

Then his sharp eyes caught sight of something else. Far away, on the beach across the bay, a fishing boat was moored and some men were coming down to the edge of the sea in a group. Mustapha knew what that meant – a net to be pulled in. He might get some breakfast yet! Slipping off his cloak, he tied it round himself and began running along the firm sands, the gulls rising up in front of him screaming, his bare feet leaving a track behind him.

He arrived panting to find them all in rather a bad mood. They had been quarrelling over the price of the catch, and two boys had gone off, refusing to work. Mustapha had arrived at just the right time.

"I'll pull with you," he panted, standing up very straight, "and help you to carry it up to the market."

He sounded a little too keen. The fisherman realised that the boy was desperate for work and would probably take anything. He mentioned a very small sum. Mustapha's eyes flashed.

"It's too little!" he protested angrily.

"All right – forget it!" replied the fisherman, rolling up his sleeves. "There are other boys about."

There were, too. Already they were running along the beach and Mustapha had to decide quickly. He must either accept such meanness or go hungry. Scowling with rage, he flung his old cloak on the sands and took his place at the rope. The other men fell into line and at a word from the fisherman they all hauled together.

The drawing in of a net is a beautiful sight.

Men, boys and little children strain backwards, the muscles of their brown limbs taut and rippling, their heels digging deep into the sand. Then, altogether, they relax and clasp the rope further down before the next great pull. They work in silence, to a perfect rhythm, adding their little strength to the might of the incoming tide, and the net, far out at sea, is brought in to the shore. Then, with a last great heave and a sudden shout, the net is landed and a frenzied mass of silver fish writhes on the sand, sparkling in the sunshine, while the men run forward to examine and sort the catch. Much of it is no good, and is thrown on one side in a bright heap of red starfish and orange jelly-fish. But the sardines, the octopuses, the herrings and the mackerels are piled into flat wooden boxes which drip at the joints, and the boys carry them on bowed shoulders to market, their clothes becoming soaked with fishy salt water.

Mustapha seized a box of sardines, for other boys were eager for the job as well as himself. In fact, they were quarrelling already and he thought it better to go as soon as possible. He set off at a steady trot, the cold water leaking down his neck; but he was happy, for he had not long to wait for his breakfast.

It was quite a climb to the market, and his shoulders ached and his fingers were numb. But the market was full these days, for it was the season when the Christians celebrated the birth of

Christ, and all ate turkey and cakes and bought flowers and toys for their children. The stalls in the centre of the square were a blaze of coloured flowers and little potted Christmas trees. It was only eight o'clock in the morning but already the streets were crowded with French, Spanish and English shoppers with big baskets on their arms finding their last bargains. For tomorrow was Christmas.

Mustapha dumped the fish before its owner and received his payment with a scowl. It should have been far more than that; the man was a cheat and a robber of the poor! Still, Mustapha was used to that, and the coin would buy him breakfast – four fried doughnuts and a glass of coffee. He would feel better after that and he would spend the morning in the market in the hope of carrying a Christmas basket for some housewife. The day began to look brighter except that his damp tunic clung to him, and there was very little warmth in the winter sunshine. Where was his old cloak?

He suddenly remembered. He'd left it on the beach. In his haste to get away, and warm with the exercise of pulling and carrying, he had forgotten all about it.

He forgot his hunger, for to lose his cloak was about the worst thing that could happen to him. Turning his back on the market, he scudded down the streets as fast as he could and reached the sea front. The tide had come in, and the river that flowed into the sea had filled up and was quite deep. He plunged in almost up to his waist, but hardly noticed the cold for the thought of losing his cloak made him forget everything else. Eagerly he scanned the beach; yes, that was the place! There was the boat and the heap of jelly-fish and the sand churned up by their feet. But the cloak had gone.

Yes, it had gone and it was no use searching any more. There was no hope of getting another and the cold weather was just beginning. He would have to save up for a sack and he'd better start right away by going without his coffee and making do with just two doughnuts.

Bitterly angry, he wandered back towards the town. The sun was high now, and the sea a sheet of sparkling blue. Why was the morning so beautiful, and men so wicked? He had been cheated of half his wages and his cloak had been stolen. He hated everybody.

Midday

The packet boat from Gibraltar arrived at 11am, and as it came round the headland Mustapha hurried down the stone jetty that led to the port. This was usually the best hour of his day, the hour on which he depended for his dinner. The thing was to be there early, for there were many other hungry street boys who also depended on the boat from Gibraltar for their dinner and there wasn't always enough work to go round.

With the scream of sirens, the ship drew in and cast anchor. Every boy was alert as the passengers streamed through the Customs with heavy cases and heavy cargo was piled on the wharf to be lifted on to lorries. The boys would get alongside bewildered-looking tourists and offer to show them round the town, or take them to their hotels, for a fabulous price. If that failed, there were usually cases to carry.

Mustapha was not very good with the tourists. He was too thin, and his dark eyes were too sad. Tourists had not come to be reminded of poverty and hunger. They had come to enjoy themselves and they liked jolly, amusing, self-confident boys. Years of living in the lonely mountains had made him unsure of himself in crowds, but occasionally he was lucky and today he pranced up to a young lady in shorts, carrying binoculars and a camera – she was obviously over for the day and most uncertain of herself. She was silly to come alone and should be easy to persuade she needed help.

"I show you all," he chanted, using the three sentences of English that he knew, jumping about a little in a desperate attempt to seem jolly and amusing. "I very good. Hundred pesetas."

The girl hesitated and might have fallen into the trap, but a fat man, smoking a cigar, came to her rescue.

"Not a cent more than twenty, young lady," he remarked firmly, "and if I were you, I should get a proper guide. These boys are thieves and rascals."

The girl stalked off with an indignant look at Mustapha, who stood scowling. He hated the fat man in the fur-lined overcoat, with his fat cigar. What did he know about hunger? There he was, taking the girl off himself, probably to some expensive restaurant up on the Boulevard to eat a huge meal and drink and smoke. However, it was no good wasting time brooding. He must look sharp or he'd get nothing. There was a tired-looking Spanish woman with a baby and a heavy suitcase, the type who could not afford a taxi; not very profitable, but there was nothing else left. He must get all he could out of her. He rushed forward and seized the case. She gave it up and he hurried along the wharf with it.

He hadn't gone five yards before a man came running down the wharf and kissed the tired woman and took the baby in his arms. Then he reached out for the suitcase and dropped two pesetas into Mustapha's outstretched hand without looking at him; and it was no use arguing or making a row, because it was all that was reasonably due to him. The big chance of his day was over, and he'd earned two pesetas.

He loafed along the beach, watching the waves and sick of everything. It was midday. He had no heart left to rush straight back to the crowded market. He would wait a little. The beach was the only quiet place in the town, and Mustapha sometimes hungered for quietness. The city was a cruel place where every man lived for himself and the strongest and the cleverest came out on top. He suddenly longed to turn his back on it all and go back to the rocks and rivers of his mountain village. But his father and mother were dead, and there was no place for him there – nor anywhere else, he thought, staring dully at the sea.

He had reached the spot where they had hauled in the net that morning. The boat still lay on its side on the beach and a dark-eyed boy with a shaved head was sitting cross-legged on the sand, mending a net. When he noticed Mustapha he stared at him closely.

"Were you on the net this morning?" he asked.

"Yes," said Mustapha, not really interested.

"So was I," said the boy, "I saw you. Did you lose your cloak?"

"Yes," said Mustapha, suddenly eager. "Where is it?"

The boy threw a pebble in the air and caught it. He was silent for a moment.

"What will you give me if I tell you?" he asked cautiously.

Mustapha felt desperate. "I have nothing to give you," he cried. "I haven't had any dinner yet, and the fisherman cheated me over my wages. Tell me where it is and I'll pay you another day."

The fisher lad shook his head shrewdly. It was a land where no boy would trust another boy.

"One peseta," he bargained, "and I'll show you the house. The man who stole it has gone out with the boats and won't be home for a couple of days. There's only a woman there. You can just take it. I live next door and I saw him carry it off."

He went quietly on with his work without looking up. Mustapha flung the peseta down on the sand beside him and the boy rose to his feet.

"Come on," he said, gathering up the net, "follow me!"

They hurried up the beach and over the railway line to the salt meadows. There, sea water was stored in hollows and ditches, and as it evaporated under the scorching summer sun the deposit of salt was left behind. But in the winter the meadows were dry and the only signs of life were a few ragged children playing round a cluster of huts, where fishermen and salt-makers lived.

"That's it," said the boy very quietly, giving a nod towards the smallest hut. "Goodbye, and may God help you!"

He disappeared into his own home and Mustapha hesitated a moment. He felt rather frightened, but anger made him bold. Marching to the door he knocked loudly and stuck out his chest, trying to look manly.

There was silence for a moment, then a weak voice said, "Come in."

It was a very bare room and rather dark. In one corner lay a pile of fishing tackle and a baby donkey, and in the other lay a young woman on a straw mat, hugging a clay pot of ashes and moaning a little. A neighbour sat beside her and at their feet tossed a restless little figure covered with Mustapha's cloak.

Ha! The boy had spoken the truth. This was the den of thieves and now he had caught them! He would seize his cloak and threaten them with the police till they cried for mercy. Not that he intended to carry out his threat, for Mustapha's whole life was spent avoiding the police and it would be a great mistake to have anything to do with them at all. Still, it would sound good.

"Where's the man who stole my cloak?" he shouted gruffly. "You'd better hand it over quickly and pay me for having taken it, or the police will be here in half an hour. Do you hear me?"

The young woman turned her head wearily. She seemed to be thinking of something else. Mustapha realised that she had taken very little notice, and his loud, gruff voice sounded foolish and cheap. The tired mother and the sick child had neither the heart nor the strength to resist him. The neighbour, a worn old granny, just stared at him, for it was none of her business. Only the baby donkey seemed frightened and backed into its corner.

"Take it," said the young woman, lifting her head and pointing to the little heap at her feet. "My husband has gone out with the boats. He won't be home till tomorrow night. I have no money in the house."

She turned her face to the wall and shut her eyes. There was nothing left to do but to take it. Mustapha dragged it roughly off the child who cried and shivered, as though woken suddenly from a restless dream. Even Mustapha could see that it was a very sick child. The old neighbour rose up slowly, with great difficulty, and carried the feverish little child to its mother's side and laid it under the cotton gown that covered her. Perhaps her arms would keep it warm.

No one spoke. There was nothing to do but to go away. As he left the hut, the cloak over his arm, a cloud blew across the sun and dark shadows settled over the sea.

Back along the beach, Mustapha was feeling almost faint with hunger. Today he had won a victory and got his cloak back, but instead of feeling happy he felt miserable and wretched, and wondered why.

Afternoon

Mustapha bought a hunk of bread and two fried sardines and looked round for some company.

He did not want to be alone. He wanted anyone or anything that would make him forget the quiet room, the smell of fishing tackle, the white-faced woman and the sick child. He joined a group of street boys lounging on the pavement by the bus stop, and sat down to enjoy his dinner as best he could.

The shoe-shine boys were doing well, for everyone wanted to be smart for Christmas. They had been up in the market and were full of stories, for this feast was an interesting time of year – so much food in the shop windows, and the buyers seemed to be particularly generous.

"What do these Christians *do* at this feast of theirs?" asked one tall boy.

"They eat turkey," replied a scruffy-looking boy who was lounging against a wall. "I used to work for one of them. And they get drunk, too, and smoke many, many cigars, and give presents to their children. It is a wonder how much they eat! But they never offered me any. I was only the gardener's boy."

He turned and spat on the ground as a sign of disgust.

"But *why* do they keep this feast?" asked the tall boy again. He seemed interested.

"They say it's the day their prophet Jesus was born," replied another lad. "They say he is the Son of God."

"I know all about it," added a third lad eagerly. "I've been up in the Christian hospital.

I stayed in four days and at night they came and preached their religion. They tried to make us learn: 'God loved the world so much that he gave his only Son.'"

He mimicked the voice of the foreign speaker perfectly, and they all roared with laughter at his performance.

"Some listened and even repeated the words because they thought they would get better treatment," he continued. "However, I must say that doctor was kind. He treated us all alike, whether we listened or not, and he made no favourites of the rich."

The talk moved on to other subjects. The shoe-shine boys returned to the market, but Mustapha and a few others lingered on, for a long-distance bus would be coming soon and then there might be work for one or two of them. The afternoon was drawing on. The ex-gardener's boy put his hand in his pocket and gave a loud exclamation. His pocket had been picked.

Furiously he set on the nearest boy, who happened to be Mustapha. The lad struggled, but his cloak was dragged off his back, and he was cuffed into silence while they searched him. Finding him innocent, they pushed him aside and made off to find a policeman to round up the shoe-shine boys.

Mustapha, bruised and shaken, decided to get as far away as possible. He made for his one and only refuge, the seashore, and for the third time that day he tramped by the edge of the waves, sick at heart.

For a long time he did not look up. What a miserable day it had been! All days weren't like that. Some days the sun shone; they laughed and joked and managed to make money, and then there was food and shelter. But, when he really thought about it, they nearly always laughed because someone had been hurt or cheated or robbed. Today, on that deserted beach, Mustapha suddenly seemed to see things as they were, and hated all the greed and spitefulness and fear and quarrelling and uncleanness that made up their daily lives. Tired and bruised, he flung himself down on the sand and stared at the sea.

He looked up. The soft colours of the sky were reflected in the water. A gull rose towards the last light on shining wings. Why had they spoiled the world like this? And was there any escape from such a miserable existence? He did not know. He had never really thought about it before.

Then he suddenly remembered bits of the conversation by the bus stop. He remembered quite clearly because they used words he had rarely heard. "God so loved that he gave..."

Loving ... giving ... peace. Those words seemed like three bright signposts in a wilderness – words that, as yet, meant almost nothing to Mustapha and his gang. Hating, grabbing, fighting – that was their code; but it did not lead to any way of peace.

And yet Mustapha had known about these words in years past. His mother had loved him and given, given, given until she had nothing left at all. And Mustapha remembered that she had lain down at peace on the night she died. It was snowing, and she had wrapped him in the only warm covering in the house – his precious cloak. It was the last thing she had to give.

What was *peace*? Early summer mornings on the mountains, sunset over the sea ... loving ... giving. But he had frightened a helpless woman and stripped the covering from a sick child. Suddenly, quite clearly, he knew where his own path of peace lay and he turned his head to look at it.

Like someone in a dream he got up and made his way to the door of the fisherman's hut. It was not locked, for the neighbour was returning later and had left it on the latch. Mustapha opened it very softly without knocking and stepped inside.

A little lamp was burning and all was quiet except for the heavy breathing of the sick child – but Mustapha knew at once that something had happened. The young woman was propped up on a pillow looking down at the new baby she held at her breast, and her tired face was peaceful, for she too was loving and giving.

It must have been born soon after Mustapha left, for the room was clean and tidy and the baby washed. The little donkey had drawn close and stood watching on long wobbly legs, and the sick child tossed and moaned under the cotton covering. Then the woman suddenly looked up and saw Mustapha standing shyly in the doorway.

She gave a cry of fear and would have beaten on the wall to call her neighbour, but Mustapha ran forward.

"Don't be afraid," he said, "I'm not going to hurt you. I came to lend you my cloak – just for tonight, because your child is ill. Tomorrow I must take it back, but I'll try and bring you a sack. Tonight, at least, she shall keep warm."

He stooped and covered the little girl and the woman looked at him curiously. When he had come before he had stuck out his chest and shouted and swaggered like a man, but now as he stood there, humbly, she realised that he was only a young boy, fourteen at the most – a child really, and not yet hard or wicked.

"Sit down," she said in a weak voice, "the teapot is on the fire. Pour yourself out a glass."

He huddled over the dying charcoal and eagerly drank a glass of hot, sweet mint tea. It was days since he'd tasted any.

"Why did you bring it back?" asked the woman, still very puzzled.

"Hakada," Mustapha replied, which is a convenient way of saying, "What is, is, but I couldn't give any reason for it if I tried." He couldn't understand himself what had made him do such a thing.

"Where do you live?" went on the woman.

"Nowhere," answered the boy. "I've only been here three years. I came down from the mountain villages."

"Why, so did I," said the woman eagerly. "My husband brought me down when I married him seven years ago and I've never been back since. What village do you come from?"

Mustapha named his village. It was only a few miles from hers on the eastern side of the same mountain. They had travelled the same paths, picked olives, grapes and figs on the same slopes, and burned charcoal among the same rocks. She was too tired to talk much, but Mustapha was glad to pour out his homesick heart to her, for in three years she was the first person he had met who knew his village.

He chatted on about the seasons back home and he was back again in thought on his mountain, a happy child, running up the rocks after the goats, and coming home to his mother at night. He talked and talked, and she lay and listened, occasionally asking a few questions. But she was not as homesick as he was, for her children had been born in this hut on the salt flat and her heart was now here with them. Home to her was the baby in her arms and the child who lay tossing at her feet.

The little girl gave a sudden sharp cry, and the

mother dragged herself painfully forward to quieten her. She had woken and wanted water. She held a glass to her lips and she drank feverishly and wept with little gasping sobs to come into her arms. She laid the new baby on the floor and dragged the sick child towards her.

"What is the matter with her?" asked Mustapha.

"I don't know," answered the woman, rocking her wearily to and fro. "She has been ill for three days. Each day I ask my husband to take her to the hospital, but he does not love her because he wanted a boy, and he always says he hasn't time. I am too weak to go, so I suppose she will die, but if I could carry her to the doctor she would live."

"How do you know?" asked Mustapha.

"I took her before," explained the woman simply. "She had fever, as she has now, and could neither suck nor breathe. The doctor gave her the needle and her fever went away. He would do it again, for he is a kind man, but who can carry her? We have no money to ask him to come here."

Mustapha thought for a moment. Then he said, "I will carry her. I know where the hospital is."

The woman looked at him, wondering if she could trust him. She was a simple woman who knew very little about sickness, and she was desperately afraid her child would die. She did not like sending her out by night in the cold, but she had great faith in the needle and thought this was probably her only chance. As for Mustapha, the fact that he came from her district made her more prepared to trust him.

The little girl, finding herself safe in her mother's arms, had fallen asleep and did not wake when Mustapha picked her up. They wrapped her in the cloak, and nodding goodbye he set off quickly across the salt flats. The moon was coming up over the sea, making a silver track across the waves, and Mustapha was glad of its light for he had quite a long way to go. The child lay with her head on his shoulder and the pressure of her burning little body kept him warm. He took the short cut back along the beach; the tide was out and the stretches of sand glistened in the moonlight. There was no one else about at all, just him and his little burden. Once or twice she stirred and whimpered, but he soothed her and rocked her a little, and whispered tender words he had heard himself long ago and almost forgotten. If only she gets better! he thought.

He had almost reached the pier now, and would have to head up through the town. The market would be a blaze of noise and colour tonight, but Mustapha had no wish to leave the beach. Here on the silver sands he felt peaceful, as though there was healing and forgiveness in the Christmas moonlight.

He did not know why he felt peaceful. He

didn't realise it was because he, Mustapha, was loving and giving.

Evening

The market on Christmas Eve was a grand sight, the stalls glittering with lighted Christmas trees and shop windows blazing. The place swarmed with rich children out for walks in their best clothes, seeing the sights with their parents. There were also wretched beggars, some blind and deformed, hoping the Christmas shoppers were feeling generous enough to throw them something. Mustapha's friends were all there too, and on any other night Mustapha would have been among them, enjoying the fun, looking for opportunities to steal. But tonight he had an important job to do and he did not want to meet his friends. He chose the more deserted back streets and hurried on past the town centre up the cobbled steps that led to the hospital on the top of the cliff.

He wondered whether the doctor might be celebrating with the rest, or even drunk. Mustapha was weak from hunger and the hot baby in his arms seemed to grow heavier and heavier. He hoped he had not come for nothing.

He reached the gates that led to the hospital compound and he hesitated, wondering which way to go. Then a man of his own race crossed the garden between the houses and Mustapha went up to him bravely and shyly asked for the doctor.

"He's in the house," said the man, jerking his thumb over his shoulder, "but he's busy."

"But this little girl is very ill," pleaded the boy. "I've brought her a long way."

The man glanced at her and heard the heavy breathing. He shrugged his shoulders. "You'd better go and see," he said. "Knock at the door and show him the child."

Mustapha crept on. The door of the house was shut, but light streamed from the windows and there was the sound of music and laughter from within. The boy hesitated. No doubt they were celebrating, and perhaps they would all be drunk after all. But no; as he listened he realised that the sounds he had heard were the laughter and shouting of little children. Perhaps, after all, a little child would be welcome here.

So he knocked and stood ready to run away in case things turned out badly.

The doctor himself opened the door. He looked flushed and his hair was standing on end, but he was not drunk. He had just been playing musical chairs and he carried his own fat, rosy son of three in his arms.

He stood blinking at Mustapha for a moment, his eyes unused to the darkness. He saw a boy with a white, hungry, dirty face and dull eyes, very thin and dressed in a cotton gown that had once been white. In his arms he carried an unhealthy-looking baby wrapped in a ragged cloak.

"She's ill," said Mustapha, and held her out.

The doctor, who was also a father, put his own son down in the passage, where he toddled off to rejoin the party. Then he stretched out his arms and took in his place the other baby, thin, dirty and sick, and carried her into the warmth and light of his own home. Years later, Mustapha often remembered that moment, for it showed him the whole meaning of Christmas – a father, a son, the dark night outside and the needy child welcomed in.

The doctor fetched some things from his study and then sat down in the passage and listened to the child's chest with a strange tube. He took her temperature, which made her scream and reach out for Mustapha, whom she had decided to trust. She was ill, but not as ill as the mother had feared – just a very bad cold and a touch of bronchitis. He would take her across to the hospital, and the nurse would give her the needle that Mustapha had shyly suggested, and then she could go home again. He told Mustapha to wait in the passage till he returned.

Mustapha sat quietly listening to the noise within and wondering where all these children came from. Surely they could not all belong to the doctor! Never before had he heard little children laugh so much or sound so happy. Then someone came out and he craned his neck to get a glimpse inside the room, and what he saw surprised him. They were mostly children of his own race – little girls in long dresses and dark plaits, and little boys with shaved heads and baggy trousers, all eating cake.

The doctor returned with the howling baby. Mustapha bowed and kissed his hand, and held out his arms for the little girl, who went to him willingly. He must get her back quickly.

But the doctor had not quite finished. He saw a great deal of poverty every day, but seldom had he seen anything as pinched and wretched-looking as this boy. And it was Christmas Eve.

"Just a moment," he said, "she'll need another injection tomorrow. Where does she live?"

"Down on the salt flats on the road to the lighthouse," answered the boy. "She can't come again. Her father won't bring her. He's away today."

"And who are *you*?" asked the doctor. "Her brother? Why can't you bring her?"

"I'm not her brother," said Mustapha simply, "I'm nobody; just a street boy. Her father will not let me bring her once he comes back."

"And her mother?" enquired the doctor. "Why doesn't she come?"

"She had a new baby this afternoon," explained Mustapha. "She is still too weak."

"Very well," said the doctor, "I'll go myself. You must show me the house now. I have to visit a man outside the town and it's not much farther to drive on to the salt fields. Come along!"

Mustapha beamed. He had never travelled in a private car before, and he was thrilled. He wanted to start at once, but once more the doctor held him back.

"And you," he said, "you look very cold. Haven't you got a cloak?"

"This is my cloak," replied Mustapha. "It is round the little girl."

"And is there no blanket to wrap her in?"

"No; the baby born this afternoon was wrapped in the blanket. She has no other."

"Then I think you had better leave your cloak to keep her warm. I think I can find you something else."

He ran upstairs two steps at a time and Mustapha waited, quite dazed. Whatever was going to happen next? Surely it couldn't mean that the doctor was going to give him clothes? But he did! Among the Christmas gifts for the hospital was a bundle of old clothing. There was a warm coat and sweater just right for Mustapha, and little woolly coats for the fisherman's children. He pulled them out and ran downstairs feeling very pleased.

"See," he said, holding them up. "These will keep you warm."

Mustapha stared, dumb and unbelieving. He did not understand this sort of thing. Perhaps the doctor was trying to sell them ... but perhaps he wasn't.

"I have no money," he whispered uncertainly.

"That's all right," said the doctor. "It's a present. We all give presents at our feast."

He held the baby while Mustapha struggled into his new clothes. They were old and repaired, but warm, and Mustapha felt like a prince in them. He had never had such clothes before. Then, rather clumsily, between them they managed to dress the baby, who was screaming again.

"Now come along," said the doctor, but as he passed the room on the left he popped his head in to say goodbye to the party that was about to break up. He came out with a handful of nuts and sweets and biscuits.

"There," he said, holding them out. "You shall share our party."

Mustapha wasn't sure whether life was real any longer or not. He found himself whizzing through the lighted streets, warm and cosy, and nibbling sugar biscuits. Soon they were speeding along the straight lighthouse road – it was wonderful!

They went straight to the fisherman's hut, and the doctor was glad he had taken the baby home because the scene there was so like Bethlehem that it made Christmas seem more real. The hut was so poor that it might well have been a stable, with the little donkey asleep now on a heap of straw, and the woman, young, tired and a stranger, with the new baby at her breast.

She was waiting anxiously for Mustapha's return, but had not expected him so soon. She looked a little worried as the doctor entered, for she had no money in the house till her husband came home, and she knew he would not be at all pleased if there was a bill to pay. But she smiled when they laid the little girl down beside her, none the worse for her adventures.

"There," said the doctor, "she's had her needle and she'll be all right. Keep her warm and give her plenty to drink and I'll be in tomorrow. Look – wc have put a woolly coat on her, and here's one for her brother."

"But I have no money," said the woman nervously, knowing that doctors usually charge a fee for a visit.

"That's all right," said the doctor. He was kneeling on the mud floor, peering at the tiny, crumpled newcomer blinking at him from the folds of the blanket. He had forgotten about thc fee – no one paid anything at Bethlehem.

Mustapha followed the doctor out into the starlight. They crossed the flats by the light of his torch. It was getting late, and he wanted a lift back into town.

"Where do you sleep?" asked the doctor as the lamps of the city came into sight round a bend in the road.

The boy hesitated. He had not yet decided where he would sleep. The cafés all seemed pretty dreary after the strange experiences of that evening. He suddenly realised that he had got to go back from this new world that he had entered for a few moments, where men loved and gave and little children laughed and played. Tomorrow he would grab and steal and fight and swear again, and those three different hours would all seem like a dream.

"I don't know," he said at last, in rather a desolate voice. "Drop me in the market."

"I know somewhere where you can spend the night," said the doctor kindly. "There's a woman near the hospital who keeps a room for boys. No – there's nothing to pay. She does it because she wants to help them. She'll let you have a blanket. We'll go along and ask her."

The doctor's visit took only a few minutes and very soon they were speeding up the hill again. They stopped in front of a little house in a narrow street near a water pump. By the light of a lamp women and girls were still filling their buckets and they called out friendly greetings to the doctor, who seemed to be well known.

He knocked at the door and it was opened by a cheerful-looking woman with a baby in her arms. At the sound of the doctor's voice the whole family ran to the door and urged him to come in and have supper with them. He entered, and they all sat down again round the bowl of steaming mush and the charcoal pot – father and mother, grown-up daughters, a baby and five scruffy street boys like himself. Mustapha recognised some of them, for they were all mountain boys, like him, driven down to the streets of the town by hunger and homelessness. He had often wondered where they slept at night. Now he knew.

The family itself was from the mountain tribes. Their house was small, poorly furnished but clean, and the boys had a room to themselves on the roof. They were all pleased to see the doctor, and the family smiled welcomingly at Mustapha, but the boys stared suspiciously. They were a gang, and another member meant less room, and probably meant less supper.

"I've brought you a Christmas present," said the doctor, his hand on Mustapha's shoulder, "a new boy."

"Welcome," replied the women, and they moved up to make room for him at the pot. Mustapha shyly took his place, and one of them broke her piece of bread in two and handed him a scoop. It was the simple food of the very poor, but to Mustapha it tasted delicious.

"And now," said Zohra, the mother, "as it is Christmas Eve, you must read to us."

She fetched a book from the shelf, and put it in the doctor's hands and he began to read. The boys already looked half asleep, warm and satisfied, but the women listened intently, and Mustapha listened too, as he'd never listened before. For the doctor read of a young woman and an outcast baby lying in a manger, and Mustapha thought of the fisherman's hut. Then he read about shepherds (Mustapha had been a shepherd himself once) and the angels' song.

"Unto you is born *a Saviour* ... Glory to God in the highest, on earth peace, goodwill toward men."

Very simply, the doctor spoke about those words. *A Saviour*, Jesus, whom God gave because he loved the world.

On earth, peace. The peace of the heart that knows forgiveness for doing wrong; the peace of a life given to that Saviour.

Goodwill – coming from the love of God that makes Christians see everyone as members of the same family. *Goodwill*, that makes them open their hearts and homes, and help and serve and give.

Mustapha sat cross-legged on the floor, his eyes fixed on the doctor's face. The little that he understood explained a lot. He knew now why the little sick girl had been accepted and cared for, why he had been clothed and fed, why he had been welcomed in out of the dark and given a shelter.

It was all quite confusing. He was beginning to feel drowsy. Zohra was telling the boys to take him upstairs and give him a blanket. The doctor had given him a pat on the head and gone home to his family.

Outside the stars shone brightly for Christmas

Eve, and all over the world Christians remembered that Christ had been born. Jesus – who brought good news to the poor, healed the broken-hearted and set people free from sadness and fear.

In the dens and sad, bad places of the city, hundreds slept and woke as usual, neither knowing nor caring.

But Mustapha was beginning to understand the glorious truth of the Christmas story, and to feel the peace of God in his young heart, which meant he would never again need to feel lonely or afraid. His future was bright, and full of hope...

The Guest

The Visit

The old woman woke with a start. Already rays of sunlight were piercing the cracks in the walls, and the hens were making a terrible noise outside. It was broad daylight, and Yacoots had overslept.

She got up slowly and stiffly. There was so much to do in the next couple of hours but it was impossible to think with the hens making that noise. There must be something the matter with them. She hobbled to the door and the cold air hit her like a blow, so that she closed her eyes for a moment as the hens rushed up to her, squawking. When she opened her eyes and looked up, it was too late. A small ragged figure was dodging up the mountainside, in and out of the olive trees on nimble feet. She glanced into the hen-house and saw that the nesting box was empty.

It was the second time that this had happened and her eyes filled with helpless tears. She did not know who the small thief was, but something must be done about it quickly because she depended on her eggs to earn her living. She could still manage the journey to market with them, although it exhausted her getting back up the hill. Sometimes she wondered how much longer she could go on alone. She needed help badly, but nobody cared. Her only daughter was married to a rich shopkeeper and he was thoroughly ashamed of his ragged old mother-in-law, although he gave her a little money now and again.

Muttering to herself, Yacoots put her water pot on her shoulder and set out for the well. The day was warming up now, and she lifted her wrinkled old face to the sunshine and felt better. It was spring, and the pink almond blossom was out. Although her old eyes were rather dim, the beauty all around her cheered her up. She forgot the thief and only remembered that in two hours Nadia would arrive and she would hear the words of the book, which were the words of God.

The bucket was heavy and she was tired when she reached the door of the hut, but there was no time to lose. Everything must be ready. She put the kettle to boil on the charcoal fire, and then she kneaded the bread and put it to rise, washed her floor, shook out the rush mat, fed the hens and polished her precious brass tray. She would not eat or drink till Nadia came, for she could not afford to do so twice. But her joy made her strong, and she worked eagerly and swiftly, for Friday's housework was different – she was preparing for a feast.

When everything was ready she placed her low round table in the sunshine of the doorway, placed the coffee pot and glasses on it, then pulled out the box from under her bed and took out the book, touching it gently with trembling fingers. It was a shabby little book with a faded paper cover, and she had had it for fifteen years.

Yacoots was not a mountain woman. She had been brought up and married in the town by the Mediterranean Sea, and had given birth to a little daughter, called Anisa.

But her husband had left her when the child was still small, and she had gone to work with a Spanish lady who had been very good to her. They could not communicate much, as neither knew much of the other's language, but she remembered her kindness and gentleness. It seemed to come from God and have something to do with the book that the lady read every night with her children at bedtime. Sometimes she tried to tell Yacoots about it, but Yacoots never understood much. She only knew it had something to do with love, and when she dusted the room and no one was looking, she would dare to lay her hand on it.

The Spanish lady's husband had paid for Anisa to go to school, and when she was fifteen she had married a country merchant and gone to live in the mountains. She had had many sons while Yacoots stayed on in the town, until one day her beloved mistress told her that they were going back to Spain, and she must find another home.

It had been the greatest sorrow of her rather sad life. The Spanish lady's children were like her own, and when the time came to say goodbye, she was full of grief, hardly noticing the lovely presents they had given her. Only one thing comforted her. Just before they left, her mistress called her and put a small paper book into her hand, written in Yacoots's own language.

"This is part of the book we read every day," she had explained. "It tells about Jesus and the way to God. Keep it carefully, and when your grandchildren grow older, ask them to read it to you. It is the word of God."

They left the same afternoon, and Yacoots went to the port and waved them off with tears streaming down her face. Then she had gone home, packed her box with her book at the bottom, wrapped in a handkerchief, and joined her daughter in her home in the mountains.

But the home was small, the boys rough and noisy, and her son-in-law did not want her. It was soon quite clear that there was no room for her, but her mistress had left her some money. Between them they had bought the hut and the patch of land, and there she had lived for fifteen years with her hens and her vegetables, and the only great event in her life had been the birth of her grand-daughter Nadia, twelve years ago.

She had never shown her book to anyone until a short time ago, and of course she could not read a word. Anisa and the boys would have laughed at the idea of an old woman like her wanting to read anything. But on that great day when her grandson came speeding through the olive trees calling, "Come – mother's had a girl," she had known things would be different in the future. Bending over the cradle, looking deep into Nadia's wise dark eyes, her heart had told her that one day she and her grand-daughter would read the book together, and then she would hear the voice of God.

She had waited patiently, never hurrying, and the child had loved her from the very beginning. When Nadia was ill or sad, it was Granny she cried for, and her mother, busy with the home and her sons, called her mother and was glad to have someone who could give all her attention to her delicate little daughter. Yacoots gave up her hens for those first six years, and became nurse to the little girl. Then Nadia went to school, and she returned home to her old life, but with one difference – on Sundays she always went to her daughter's house, and on Fridays Nadia always came to visit her.

Nadia grew tall and beautiful. She brought her school books every week to show off her progress, and at twelve years old she could read fluently in two languages. And one day, about four months ago, with a beating heart and trembling hands, Yacoots had brought out the book and told Nadia about her Spanish mistress and her gift. "It is about God and love," she had said rather vaguely. "For fifteen years it has been hidden in my box. I have never been able to read it."

And Nadia, who had no books except her school books and who loved reading, was thrilled. She sat down at once to study it, becoming quite absorbed by the story. Yacoots, watching her intently, would never forget that picture. Nadia sat reading in the doorway in the pale winter sunshine, and when at last she looked up, her dark eyes were shining.

"It's a good book, Granny," she said. "We will read it together. Every week I will read you a chapter." After she had kissed her Granny and gone home, Yacoots had sat for a long time staring out into the sunset and the dusk, repeating the words from the book that had stuck fast in her mind: "You will call his name Jesus because he shall save his people from their sins." From that day on, Jesus had become a person – a friend who cheered her lonely little hut. She did not know who he was, nor that he had died and risen again. But something inside her made her believe that he was an important, living person. And every Friday, through the book, he spoke to her again.

The Jewel

"Hello Granny, it is not yet midday, and you are fast asleep."

Yacoots jerked herself awake and focused on Nadia standing in the doorway. She had not been asleep, only dreaming about the past. Her grand-daughter was laughing and flushed with running, and they greeted each other warmly, happy to be together again.

They always began their Fridays with breakfast. Yacoots could not afford coffee very often and brewed it very carefully, to drink with the bread, hot from the pan, while Nadia sat cross-legged on the mat and told her all the news of the week. She was a merry, lively child, and described things very vividly. Their neighbourhood had had a new baby, and Nadia had been considered old enough to go to the Seventh-day feast, and her father had given her a long blue embroidered dress covered in white lace – yes, she would dress up in it on Sunday for Granny's benefit. Her brothers were quarrelling because they wanted new clothes too, but their father said they must wait. The floods had carried away part of the river bank and two goats had been drowned, and their owners were going to sue the town council. A thief had got in through her cousin's roof-top and stolen her golden bracelets. At this point Yacoots remembered her own thief and told Nadia about him.

"I wanted to fry you eggs for breakfast," she said sadly, "but he took them all. He was small and ragged and barefoot, and he ran very fast."

Nadia nodded gravely. "I think that would be Rachid, Granny," she said. "His father died and his mother married again and has gone away. His step-father would not have him. He roams the hills and works on farms, but he does not come near the town in case the police should put him in the poor-house. But anyone could steal your eggs, Granny. You need a big fierce dog."

"But how could I feed it? I can hardly feed myself."

Nadia could think of no way out of this difficulty. "I will ask my father," she murmured, and she sighed. It was her polite way of saying that there was really nothing to be done about the problem and there was a moment of sad silence. It always troubled Nadia that her rich father cared so little about her old granny.

But Yacoots hardly noticed, for the great moment of the day was approaching. Nadia cleared the breakfast things, Yacoots swept the crumbs, and they were ready. They drew the curtain across the doorway and settled themselves in the corner of the room, then Nadia opened the book.

"It's chapter 18 today, Granny," she announced. "Do you remember what chapter 17 was about?"

It always amused Nadia that her granny loved the book so much and yet remembered so little of it. But, really, Yacoots never tried to take in much. Nadia read in a fast, sing-song voice, and most of it flowed over her granny's head. But every week, out of the confusion of the words, the old woman remembered something precious, like a jewel, and this fed her spirit for the rest of the week. She would remember the words when she woke in the morning, and as she worked in her hut and little garden they seemed to give her strength. "Come to me all who are tired and carry heavy burdens, and I will give you rest." This had been one of her brightest jewels, because of course that meant her and her water-pots. She would murmur the words as she went to the well, and the buckets had never seemed so heavy since. And as she thought about the words, they seemed to mean more and more and seemed to lead her to God. But on Friday mornings she would put aside last week's words in the storehouse of her memory, and wait for a new word. And it was always given. The book never failed her.

She smiled at the twinkle in Nadia's eye. "Jesus climbed a mountain, and his clothes and his face shone, and God said, 'This is my Son,'" she replied. "And there was a fish with some money in its mouth."

"And what else, Granny?"

"I don't remember anything else. That was enough. All this week I have seen that brightness. It has shone in my heart like love. What more should I need to hear?"

Nadia sighed. Her granny's watery old eyes were fixed on her expectantly. She found the chapter and started to read. What a strange book of contrasts it was, she thought. One week all about the shining glory of God's voice from heaven, and the next all about little children, lost sheep and quarrelling servants. Strange that a holy book should concern itself with such ordinary things.

She did not realise that, once Granny had found her jewel, she usually stopped listening and didn't hear the end of the chapter at all. And today she found it in verses three and four – words so amazing that having heard them, Yacoots even forgot Nadia was there until her grand-daughter prodded her with her bare foot.

"Granny, didn't you listen? That was a good story about that servant, wasn't it? I think he deserved to go to prison."

"To go to prison?" Yacoots blinked vaguely. "Who went to prison, my daughter?"

"Granny!" Nadia was really shocked. "I read it so nicely and slowly and I don't believe you heard a word!"

"Indeed, I heard every word!" retorted Yacoots, equally shocked. "It was all about a little child... 'If you receive a little child, you receive me.' Now what could that mean, my child?"

But Nadia had no idea what it meant and was only really interested in the stories. She had really enjoyed the story of the unforgiving servant. She retold it all to her granny, vividly and with actions, and they discussed the rights and wrongs of it and laughed together, until Nadia noticed the long shadows of the poplar trees and jumped to her feet.

"It's nearly sunset, Granny," she said. "I must run."

She skipped to the well, refilled the bucket, kissed the old woman on both cheeks and made her promise to come on Sunday. Yacoots watched her feet running up the hill, until she disappeared among the olive trees.

And now Yacoots was alone, and this was the most special time of her week. Dearly as she loved Nadia, she also loved to be alone with the pale colours of the sky, thinking over what she had heard. She sat perfectly still in the doorway, her hands folded on her lap, staring out into the spring twilight. She felt she had discovered some tremendous new secret, some key that would open a new door. And yet the secret was a story written in words she could not understand, and the key would not fit the lock.

"Whoever receives a little child receives me... Jesus, whose name means 'God with us'." Yacoots didn't understand what it meant, but she knew that Jesus had come to her because of the peace and comfort she felt, and the sense of protection that surrounded her on winter nights when the storms shook the hut. These new words said that if she received a child, she could receive him.

But what little child? And where was he? There were dozens of children in the farms on the hill-side around her – noisy little creatures with spotty heads and runny noses, who chased her hens and trampled her garden and who made her very angry. Surely it could not mean one of these?

She grew tired of wondering and it was getting cold. The sky had clouded, and it smelt of rain and green things growing.

Tonight she would lie down and sleep and hope that tomorrow might bring the answer to her questioning. She did not know how to pray, but she could look at the stars through a hole in the thatch and hope and wish. Often something happened during the week that helped her understand her jewels.

But that night there were no stars and the rain came down in torrents. Yacoots shivered under the ragged blanket and groaned because of her rheumatism, passing the night sleeping and waking. But every time she dozed off she dreamt of a little child, with eyes like Nadia's, creeping in to find shelter from the storm.

The Child

Sometime near the dawn she fell deeply asleep and would have slept right on through the morning if she had not been woken again by a tremendous commotion in the hen-house. She could not hurry, for the wet night had affected her badly and every joint felt stiff. The rain had dripped through the hole in the thatch and the cold air made her cough and wheeze. By the time she had wrapped herself in a blanket and hobbled through the mud to the hen-house the birds had settled again, but the nesting box was empty.

Yacoots sat down painfully on the sack of grain and began to cry – weak tears of despair. She just did not know what to do. No doubt, early next morning he would come again. What was there to stop him? She could not sit there all night long, and the police would never really bother about an old woman and five eggs. If only she had a fierce dog, but how could she feed him? Never had she felt more helpless and alone. She cried out in the gloom, "I can't go on any longer, I need help."

The sound of her own quavering voice startled her. To whom had she spoken? Not to the restless, squawking hens, nor to her poor shivering self. There was someone else in the hen-house, and she somehow felt that her words had reached an ear that heard and a heart that cared. She did not know anything about prayer, and yet she had prayed. She had made her greatest discovery yet – that Jesus, who spoke to her through the book and whose presence comforted her in the wet nights, could also hear, and that thought gave her great joy. She could tell him everything for ever, all about her fears and helplessness and loneliness. It was like laying down a heavy burden.

She sat quietly for a long time, and then an idea came into her mind, so strongly that it seemed as though someone had spoken. "Get up, and go and look for the child who stole the eggs."

She thought this over for a long time, and the more she thought about it, the more sensible it seemed. What was the point of sitting there waiting to be robbed? Nadia had even said she knew the child who had done it. She would never dare go to the police herself; she had kept clear of them all her life, but surely for Nadia's sake her son-in-law would speak up for her and have the child caught and shut up where he deserved to be. She clenched her fists at the very thought of him. Of course she had never seen him, and could not actually prove who had done it but surely someone would help her.

She fed the hens hastily. Everything else could wait. Later she would mop up the water from the floor and go to the well. Nothing mattered except bringing this child to justice. Her anger strengthened her, and she needed strength because her rheumatism was very bad, and the steep path leading up to the main road through the olive groves was a river of liquid mud and the rain was still falling.

It seemed at first as though she took one step forward and two backward. Soaked through, she stumbled on, clutching at the olive boughs, leaning against their trunks. Half-way up the hill she crouched under the eaves of the deserted farm hut that stood there and rested for a while. It had been empty for so long that she did not even know who had lived there. Its mud and dung walls were crumbling and its roof almost fallen in, and it was in such a wet, draughty position that no one had ever wanted to rebuild it – a desolate place, thought Yacoots, as she sheltered from the rain.

And then she heard a sound coming from inside the shack, and it sounded as if someone was coughing.

She listened intently; something was whimpering and then coughing again. Perhaps it was a sick dog or fox, for no one could live in such a ruin. It was an eerie sound, and she gave a little shudder as, her weariness forgotten, she started off for the path. But as she slithered in the mud she stopped. The whimpering was louder, and it came from no animal. It was the unmistakable cry of a child in pain, and quite a young child, too.

Cautiously, fearfully, she paddled round to the door and peered in, ready to run if she saw anything scary. At first she could see nothing at all, but as her eyes grew accustomed to the gloom, she saw a little figure huddled in some straw, its face hidden in its sleeve. It seemed half asleep and yet coughed and whimpered in turns, and sometimes shivered. Yacoots watched it for a long time and then decided there was nothing to be afraid of. It was just a sick little boy... a child.

She stepped over the rubble and squatted down on the straw and laid her hand on the child's ragged jelab.[1] She could feel the burning

---

1 A long loose outer garment with a hood, worn by men, especially in N. Africa.

temperature of his body. He jumped violently at her touch and raised himself on his elbow, and when he saw her, he cringed away from her. He was only about nine years old, thin and very dirty, his face flushed and his eyes fever-bright.

"What is the matter, my little boy?" she asked. "Why do you lie here? Where is your home?"

He relaxed and turned towards her, his head pillowed on his arm. "I have no home," he said, "I look after sheep and I live here."

"By yourself?"

He nodded forlornly. After a pause he said, "Bring me some water." She went outside and found a piece of old broken pot and scooped rain water from a hollow. He drank eagerly and started coughing and shivering again, gazing up at her. She had thrown her own haik[2] around him, and she looked to him like some comforting angel – or like his granny, who had loved him and died. "Stay with me," he said, "don't leave me."

She stared back, thinking about his words. They reminded her of something, but she could not quite remember what. Then it came back to her – "Don't leave me ... receive me ... a little child, and you'll receive me." Perhaps this was the child she was looking for. There was no difficulty at all about how to receive this one. He

2 A large piece of cotton, silk or wool cloth, draped over the head and about the body, worn as an outer garment by Arabs.

needed shelter and food and water, and he was filthy. She jerked herself back to the practical details, but her heart was beating fast with excitement.

"Have you no parents?" she asked.

He shook his head. "My father died," he explained. "My mother married again. Her husband took her back to the village with their children. He left me with a weaver, but he beat me all day long so I ran away."

"And now?"

"I work for a shepherd. I look after his sheep and goats. He gives me food and a little money, and I sleep here. But when I tried to go to work today my head felt dizzy, so I went to sleep again."

"It is cold and wet here," said Yacoots thoughtfully. "You had better come home with me. I have a blanket and fire and food."

He made a quick movement towards her, and as he did so, three eggs rolled out from under his clothes. She suddenly realised that this was the thief she had come to look for; but, strangely enough, she was not angry any more. She picked up the eggs, found three others in the straw and tied them into her girdle while he rolled away from her and burst into tears. Of course she would not help him now. It was as though the door of Paradise had been opened and then slammed shut again in his face.

It was all most confusing. Surely the Lord

whom she was receiving had nothing to do with stolen eggs, and yet she was quite sure that this must be the child, and her only concern was to get him home as quickly as possible.

"Come," she said, "I will help you down the path. You know where my hut is."

He stared at her unbelievingly. He had learned to trust no one, and perhaps this was just a trap to hand him over to the police. Yet she looked neither angry nor cunning, just old and simple and kind, and he wanted to stay with her more than anything else in the world.

"Come," she said again, holding out her hand. "It's not raining so hard now. Let us go quickly." The boy scrambled to his feet and snuggled under the old woman's cloak, and together they slithered down the muddy path, Yacoots clutching the eggs and the boy clutching her, breathless with coughing. By the time they reached the hut he was shivering again and only too ready to collapse on her mattress and pull her blanket over him. He felt he had come home.

And now she was ready to receive her Lord. She fetched the water and all the rest of her charcoal to make a roaring, extravagant glow, and a beautiful warmth crept through the dark room. She kneaded her bread, recklessly emptied the coffee tin and fried two eggs. Tomorrow could take care of itself. Today she was entertaining a royal guest and he must have the best of everything she had. She sat beside him on the floor and fed him with hot food and drink, and bathed his burning face and hands. She even produced a bottle of cough mixture that the doctor at the hospital had once given her, giving him far too much! He glowed with happiness and warmth and wonder and fell into a restless sleep.

She stayed beside him all day, and late in the afternoon she was conscious of a strange light in the room and tiptoed outside into the fresh air. Over the mountains great purple storm-clouds were gathering, but across the valley the sun had broken through low on the horizon, turning the thin rain to silver, and right over her hut in a sweeping arch hung a perfect rainbow. She was not in the least surprised. She went in again and baked some more bread and boiled up some barley soup. Then the rain stopped, the storm clouds rolled towards the sea and the stars came out.

There was no other blanket in the house and nowhere to lie except the floor, so sleep was difficult, but Yacoots did not want to sleep. She crouched by the dying charcoal fire, sometimes dozing a little but mostly thinking about all that had happened. It didn't matter to her any longer that the child was a thief and an outlaw. A child's hands are the same all the world over, and his hands had clung to her and his eyes had pleaded with her. "Stay with me, don't leave me," he had said, and she had found her own heart echoing the words, "Stay with me, don't leave me," and she wondered again: To whom am I speaking? To the child, or to Jesus in whose name I received this child? But this was too much for her poor old brain, and she gave up.

The room was bright with moonlight, and she turned to look at the boy and noticed he was covered with cold perspiration. She realised the fever had broken out. He woke, confused, with his teeth chattering and clung to her again while she rubbed him dry with an old piece of towelling, and blew up the fire. Then she heated up the rest of the coffee and he drank it, leaning up against her in the dark. He kissed her hand and closed his eyes, and she stayed looking down at him for a time and knew that the fever had left him. At last he was sleeping deeply and peacefully.

And that peace seemed to fill the room. She had never felt anything like it before. All her wondering, fears and anxieties fell away in the presence of it, and she knew she could just lean back and rest. That peace was like a soft pillow, and she closed her eyes and slept as deeply as the child. The floor no longer seemed hard, nor the dawn cold.

When at last she woke it was to the clatter of buckets, and the child stood in the doorway against the brightness of the noonday sun. His face was pale and he still coughed, but he seemed quite recovered from his illness. He saw that she was awake and he stood watching her anxiously. He had worked so hard. Surely she would notice. Surely she could not refuse him!

She looked round, dazzled at first and then with growing astonishment, for her prayers had been answered and help had come. The room was swept and the fire burning, and fresh firewood was stacked round it to dry. Buckets of water stood in a neat row, and the hens, being quiet, had presumably been fed. The child, eager and hungry, stood looking first at her and then at his handiwork. He presented her with a basin of brown eggs.

"I will do it every morning," he pleaded, "before I go to the goats. I will bring you firewood every day from the mountain, and in the evening I will dig your garden and grow vegetables. I will fetch you water and sweep your house. I will do anything I can to help you," he said, flinging his arms out wide. Then he pulled forward the little table and sat down expectantly, laughter bubbling up in him because he felt sure he had made his point.

"There is bread left from yesterday," he reminded her, "and see, I have brought you some goat's cheese. I told the shepherd I was ill, but when we have eaten I must go back to him... until the evening?"

His voice ended in a question mark, and she realised that he was asking to stay, and this surprised her because she had taken it for granted that he wanted to stay. Surely the heavenly guest had come to stay. She started cutting the bread, and then she glanced up suddenly, almost expecting to see Jesus in shining robes with a face like light. But all she saw was a little ragged boy in filthy clothes, sitting grinning cross-legged on her floor.